NEW YORK CITY

DIAMOND DISTRICT

EMPIRE STATE BLDG.   CHRYSLER BLDG.

NEW YORK CITY   NEW YO

MY NEW YORK

Kathy Jakobsen

New Anniversary Edition

FLATIRON BLDG.

BLOOMBERG

DIAMOND DISTRICT

WOOLWORTH BLDG.   G.E. BUILDING

BROOKLYN BRIDGE

CITY

Megan Tingley Books
LB
1837
LITTLE, BROWN AND COMPANY
New York • An AOL Time Warner Company

My name is Becky, and I live near the New York Public Library. Some buildings in New York make you feel small, but walking up the steps of the library makes me feel important. It's like walking up the steps of a palace, especially if you walk exactly in the middle. There are even lion guards looking down on all the people. The library was my favorite place in New York when we first moved here. My mother painted me a map—you can see it in the front of this book. (She's an artist and she

painted all the other pictures, too.) She said that once a week, we could go wherever I wanted to, IF I could figure out how to get there. For my first Expedition, I wanted to *see* real animals. Finding a zoo on the map was easy. Knowing where *I* was *on* the map, and which way to walk to the zoo, was a little harder. . . . I finally figured it out by turning the map.

Once the map and I were both facing the same direction, finding the zoo was easy. One good thing about New York is that most of the streets are numbered in order. The numbers go up as you go north, down as you go south. It's very logical. So we just walked straight on Fifth Avenue—I knew I was going the right way because the numbers kept going up. At 64th Street, we turned left. Sometimes,

CENTRAL PARK ZOO

zoos make you feel sorry for the animals that live in them—but at this one, most of the animals aren't in cages. The penguins have rocks to climb on (and make their nests with!) and a pool to swim in. You can stand right next to the glass and see them under water. They were my favorites, but I also liked watching the insects. I saw a leaf-cutter ant bite off a leaf, then carry it all the way back to his nest!

FRIEDSAM MEMORIAL CAROUSEL

After the zoo, we explored the park and found a carousel! I chose a big black horse with a lion saddle. It wasn't like riding a real horse, but it was kind of fun anyway—the horse went up and down when the music started. I had three rides. When I bought my last ticket, the man told me that my horse was named Bubbles—I thought that was a silly name for a big black horse with a roaring lion saddle!

ANNEX ANTIQUES FAIR, 6TH AVE. AND 26TH ST.

When I wanted to get a birthday present for my friend Martin, my parents said they were going to the 26TH Street Antiques Fair and that I could look for one there. They had a lot of antique toys, like a china dog and a wooden horse, but I didn't think Martin would really like those. I did find him some old baseball cards for his collection.

D'AIUTO'S BAKERY, NEW YORK NEW YORK CHEESECAKE

On Martin's birthday, I invited him to come with me on an Expedition. First, we went to D'Aiuto's for cheesecake—his favorite dessert. My mother says D'Aiuto's has the best cheesecake in New York. Mario D'Aiuto has owned the bakery for over fifty years, and his baby picture is still on the boxes. His grandchildren work there in little aprons! Dogs were everywhere, because a fancy dog show was going on across the street. I liked the Dobermans and a little black bulldog.

After cheesecake we went to the INTREPID, a real aircraft carrier from World War II—you can see where kamikaze planes crashed into it. The fighter jets are real, too; you can climb up platforms and look inside them. It was a very cold, windy day and we had the whole huge deck almost to ourselves. Martin ran around acting and sounding like a plane until other people came out. So we went inside. We got to work the controls in a simulated cockpit with pilot and copilot seats. Martin loved it!

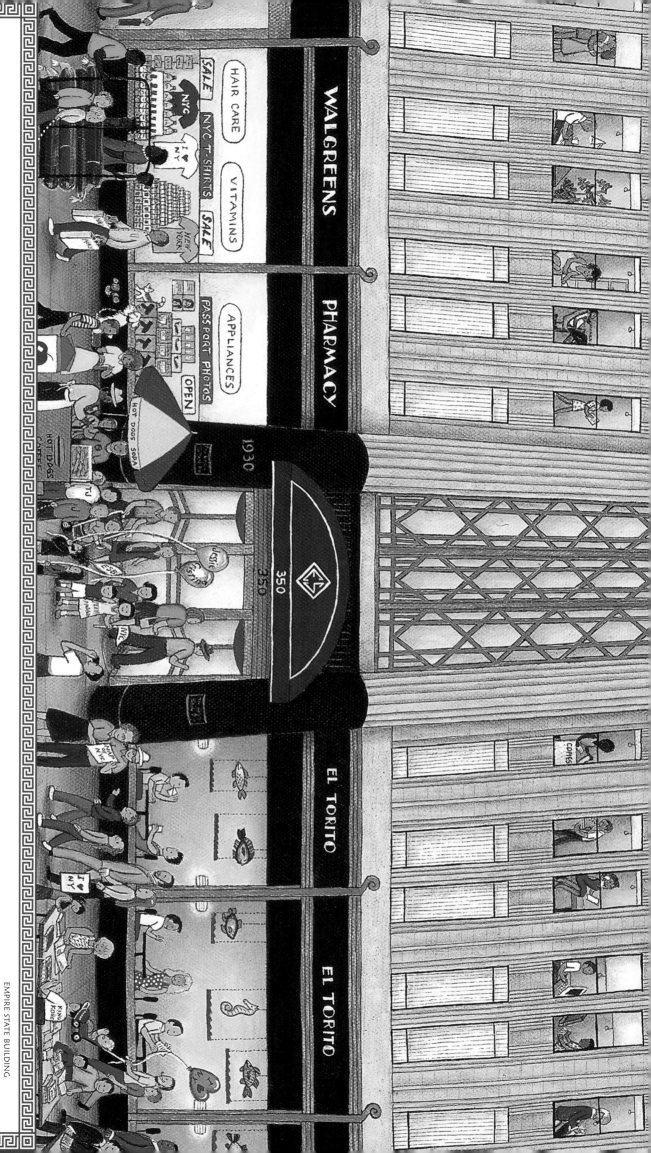

The next week, we went to the observation deck of the Empire State Building. We stepped out onto it just at that magical moment when the city and bridge lights are on, but the sky still has some of the sunset in it and it's not quite dark. You could see so far! (Turn the page and see for yourself.) In the painting, we are looking north, with the Hudson River on our left and the East River on our right. The small green square in the distance is Central Park.

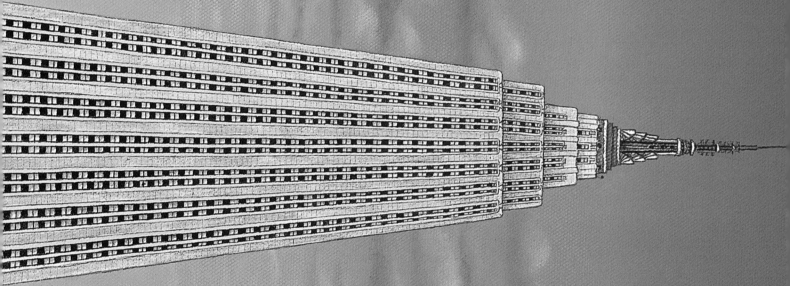

WALL STREET: NEW YORK STOCK EXCHANGE, TRINITY CHURCH, FEDERAL HALL

Martin's mother was curious about these Expeditions of ours, so for our next one, we went to Wall Street, where she works. We met her on the spot where George Washington was sworn in as our first president. In the Federal Hall National Memorial museum behind the statue, I learned that each colony had its own money. The bills were all different colors and sizes, and you can buy packs of them in the gift shop.

FAO SCHWARZ

After that, we all took the subway to my favorite toy store, FAO Schwarz. They have more stuffed animals than I've ever seen in my life—and they really are as big as my mother has painted them. She let Martin and me paint ourselves into this picture. Can you tell which are our self-portraits? I said I thought they should have toys designed by children, so she let me paint those in, too. Guess which toys I made up! (The answer is at the end of this book.)

On the Fourth of July, we went to the harbor. We saw buildings from before the Revolution and a little lighthouse memorial to the TITANIC. It has a ball on the top that drops down exactly at noon; sailors used to set their clocks by it. Then, we took a boat to the Statue of Liberty. We stopped at Ellis Island, where immigrants used to land when they came to the New World. Now it's a museum with immigrants' names on a wall and computers where people can look up their ancestors.

STATUE OF LIBERTY

I think it's neat that people still come to New York from all over the world to make new lives for themselves, and that the Statue of Liberty still welcomes them all. Inside downstairs, these words are on a plaque: GIVE ME YOUR TIRED, YOUR POOR, / YOUR HUDDLED MASSES YEARNING TO BREATHE FREE . . .

We read that and then waited on the deck for the fireworks. When it got dark, you could see two columns of light where the Twin Towers used to be.

OVERLEAF: NEW YORK HARBOR ON THE FOURTH OF JULY

GRAND CENTRAL TERMINAL

Just before school started, we spent the whole day playing in Central Park, where a kid told us that Grand Central has a whispering room. He said if we stood in opposite corners and whispered into them, we'd be able to hear each other perfectly, but no one else would be able to hear anything we said. So of course, we wanted to try it! The picture shows us running to Grand Central; behind us my mother is talking about the Chrysler Building: "It's my favorite building in New York—it's so

I saw the dinosaurs at the American Museum of Natural History with my class at school, and then again with my mother. The huge one in the painting is a barosaurus. My mother got me a postcard that tells what all the parts of dinosaurs' names mean. For example, "dino" means terrible and "saurus" means lizard. When I went with my mother, we saw the terrible lizards and then went upstairs to something I thought was even more interesting: huge extinct mammals.

CHRYSLER BUILDING

beautiful! Look!" She also told us that the ceiling of Grand Central used to be so dirty it was black. Now, it's a sky with gold stars arranged in constellations. Near Cancer the Crab they left two little squares dirty to show what the wall and ceiling used to look like. We saw them, then found the Whispering Gallery: it's near the Oyster Bar restaurant and it worked perfectly!

TREATS THE NATURAL RESOURCES
AS A ... WHICH IT MUST TURN
OVER TO THE NEXT GENERATION
INCREASED AND NOT IMPAIRED
IN VALUE

CONSERVATION MEANS DEVELOPMENT
AS MUCH AS IT DOES PROTECTION

THEODORE ROOSEVELT

Jakobsen H ©1992

BAROSAURUS, AMERICAN MUSEUM OF NATURAL HISTORY

My favorite was a giant sloth—MUCH taller than I am, and standing on its hind legs with its forelegs reaching out at you. I also liked the saber-toothed tiger teeth and the fossilized horse, which was much smaller than horses are now. The sign explaining how horses evolved said they've changed much less than many other mammals. When we were done, we decided to have a snack in the plaza on our way to the Rose Center.

ROSE CENTER FOR EARTH AND SPACE

The lights at the bottom of the plaza's fountain are arranged like the stars in Orion. Real astronomers work here, and everything is about space! The huge sphere represents the sun, and inside it are two theaters. The bottom one is the Big Bang Theater—you look down into a swirling simulation of the beginning of the universe. The top one is the planetarium—the dome darkens and stars come out the way they do in the sky at night. This isn't just a made-up show—you see the universe the way the astronomers think it really is.

We took the subway home; the stairwell has glittery stars on the tiles. I said they should have put stars on the subway ceiling, too, the way they did at Grand Central, to make it look like the night sky in the planetarium. So, my mother painted it that way—even though it's really just a plain subway ceiling. But the tile walls really do show animals on them; the extinct species are a ghostly gray.

When we got on our train we saw two Guardian Angels. These are volunteers who help people who ride the subway; they always wear red berets.

I let my mother choose the next Expedition, because it was her birthday; she chose the Metropolitan Museum of Art (she calls it the Met). I used to think art museums were boring, but this one wasn't, because of the things from ancient Egypt. The cat was a sacred animal there. We saw a goddess statue with the head of a cat and a beautiful black cat statue that opens up to hold a cat's mummy!

My parents liked the Temple of Dendur best. You walk right up to it and see hieroglyphics on the

METROPOLITAN MUSEUM OF ART

walls and graffiti that the original explorers wrote there, too. But I liked the sacred animals and the little charms, like the turquoise hippopotamus that protected a person in his next life from being attacked by *real* hippos. They have lots of other things in the Met. It's huge, but my mother believes that you enjoy museums more if you don't try to see too much on one visit.

The next week, we took the subway up to 125TH Street in Harlem. Someone was selling little sweet-potato pies right on the sidewalk and we each got one. People were selling lots of other things on the sidewalk, too—I liked the African prints because of the colors, and I liked the smell of the incense burning. But my favorite thing was the Tree of Hope. That's an elm tree that once grew in front of an

APOLLO THEATER, 125TH STREET. HARLEM

old theater; people hoping to work in show business used to touch it for luck. When the City chopped down the tree, the owners of the Apollo Theater bought the biggest slab and put it on a pillar in front of the stage. On Amateur Night people touch it for luck before they perform: it's completely smooth from so many people touching it over the years.

WASHINGTON SQUARE PARK, GREENWICH VILLAGE

During school, there was less time for Expeditions, and I didn't go on another one until Halloween. I went trick or treating with Martin, but his mother wouldn't let him come to the grown-up Halloween parade in Greenwich Village, so I went with just my parents. My mother held her hands over my eyes twice, but I got to see most of it. Which costumes do you think are the best? I vote for the two people dressed as Vikings. After the parade we walked to Chinatown for dessert.

The Chinatown Ice Cream Factory has flavors like lychee, green tea, and ginger. I chose vanilla and my mother had mango. The manager said that Thanksgiving is the most popular day for weddings and feasts; Chinatown is crowded with brides in beautiful dresses. I liked Chinatown—there were so many food smells and all the telephone booths had roofs like little temples. I wished Martin could have come, though. He would have liked seeing the live lobsters on the sidewalk.

Martin's mother did let him come to the New York City Marathon. (You can see part of the route on the map: just follow the blue line.) We held a sign for the gallery that shows my mother's paintings, because the owner was one of the runners. My mother told us that there are over 30,000 runners every year. They run through all five boroughs ("boroughs" are the five main parts of New York City).

NEW YORK CITY MARATHON

When most people say "New York," they mean the island of Manhattan, where the skyscrapers are. When people address envelopes, they put "New York, NY" for Manhattan, too. But New York City is really five boroughs: the Bronx, Queens, Brooklyn, Staten Island, and Manhattan. I live in Manhattan; Martin lives in Brooklyn—but we both live in New York City.

In New York the holidays start early. Weeks before Thanksgiving, the Christmas decorations go up and the Radio City Christmas Spectacular opens. Our parents let us take a cab to Radio City Music Hall from Martin's apartment without any grown-ups! Martin's parents put us into the cab, and my parents were waiting for us in the lobby; but it was still fun to take a cab by ourselves.

At the beginning of the show, an orchestra rose out of the floor. They played some music, and then

the orchestra went back into the floor and out came the Rockettes (women dancers who do high kicks). My favorite scene was the parade of the wooden soldiers: I loved the way they walked in like penguins and fell down at the end like dominoes. My second favorite was when a man and a woman were ice skating—they really *were* skating, on a rink with real ice. Martin's favorite was the Living Nativity, when real animals—camels, sheep, and donkeys—came out onto the stage.

The next weekend, when I first saw New York covered with deep snow, I was amazed. It made the city completely different. I had gotten used to the New York noises—suddenly, they were all gone. In the snow everything was really quiet, as though all the sounds in the city were under a spell. I HAD to go out in it, and my mother had the idea of going to Central Park and building a snow horse. So we

PLAZA HOTEL, PULITZER FOUNTAIN, GRAND ARMY PLAZA, CENTRAL PARK

did: it didn't look quite as perfect as it does in the painting, but you could tell it was a horse. On the way to the Plaza Hotel, my mother took my picture in front of the Pulitzer Fountain. They fill the fountain with Christmas trees during the holidays. (I wonder if you can still throw a coin in and make a wish when a fountain is full of Christmas trees.)

The night before Thanksgiving, you can watch people fill up the balloons for the Macy's Thanksgiving Day Parade. They close off the streets near the start of the parade and lay all the balloons out flat; then they fill them up while people watch. The night before the parade, I traced the parade route on my map. It starts at 77th Street, goes south on Central Park West, then turns onto Broadway and ends at 34th Street/Herald Square: Macy's!

That's where I decided to watch it. The balloons look even bigger in real life than they do on TV.

An old lady in the crowd told me that they used to untie the balloons at the end of the parade and let them float up into the sky—people would try to catch them or find them, and everyone who did got a reward! I think it would be fun if they still did that.

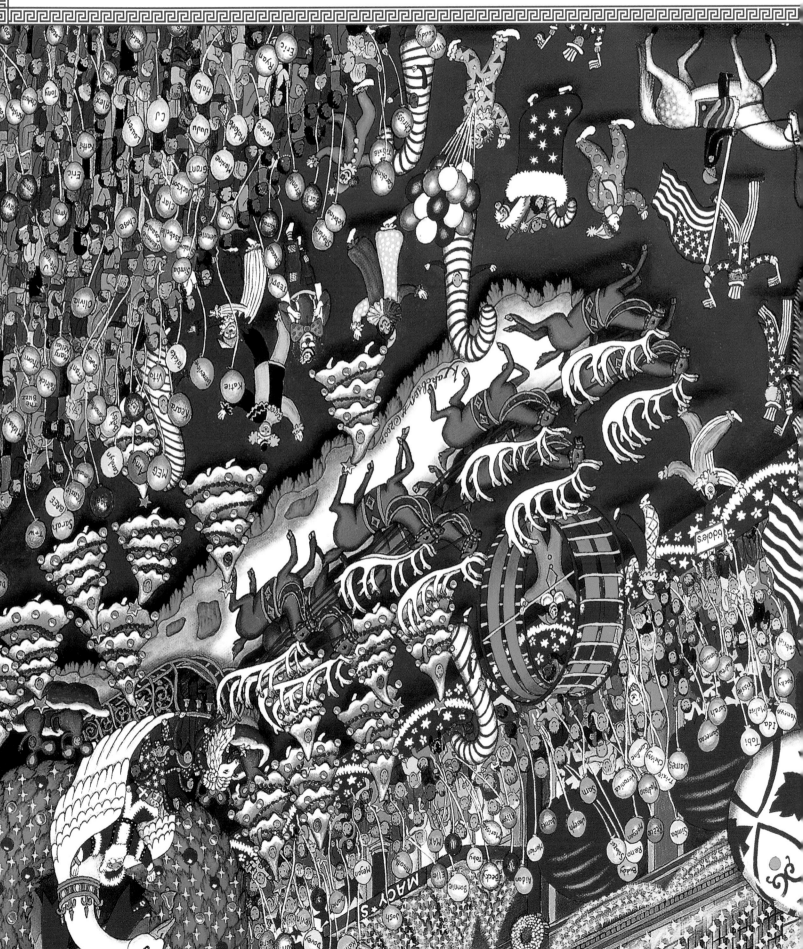

On the first night of vacation, my parents and I went to see the tree and shop for Christmas presents. (I didn't invite Martin to come because I wanted to get him a present.) Usually, I'm excited about what I'm getting, but this year I'm more excited about what I'm *giving* other people—especially Martin and my parents. Rockefeller Center was a fun place to look for presents: the buildings are all connected to each other underground by passages some people call the Catacombs.

I looked in the Met Store at Rockefeller Center for something for my mother. I found an amulet of the little turquoise hippopotamus. There was also a mummy-case puzzle that I wondered if Martin would like, but then I had a better idea. I decided to make Martin a ticket for our first Expedition of the New Year: ice skating in Rockefeller Center. (I checked the price, and I had enough money to pay for admission and rent skates for both of us.)

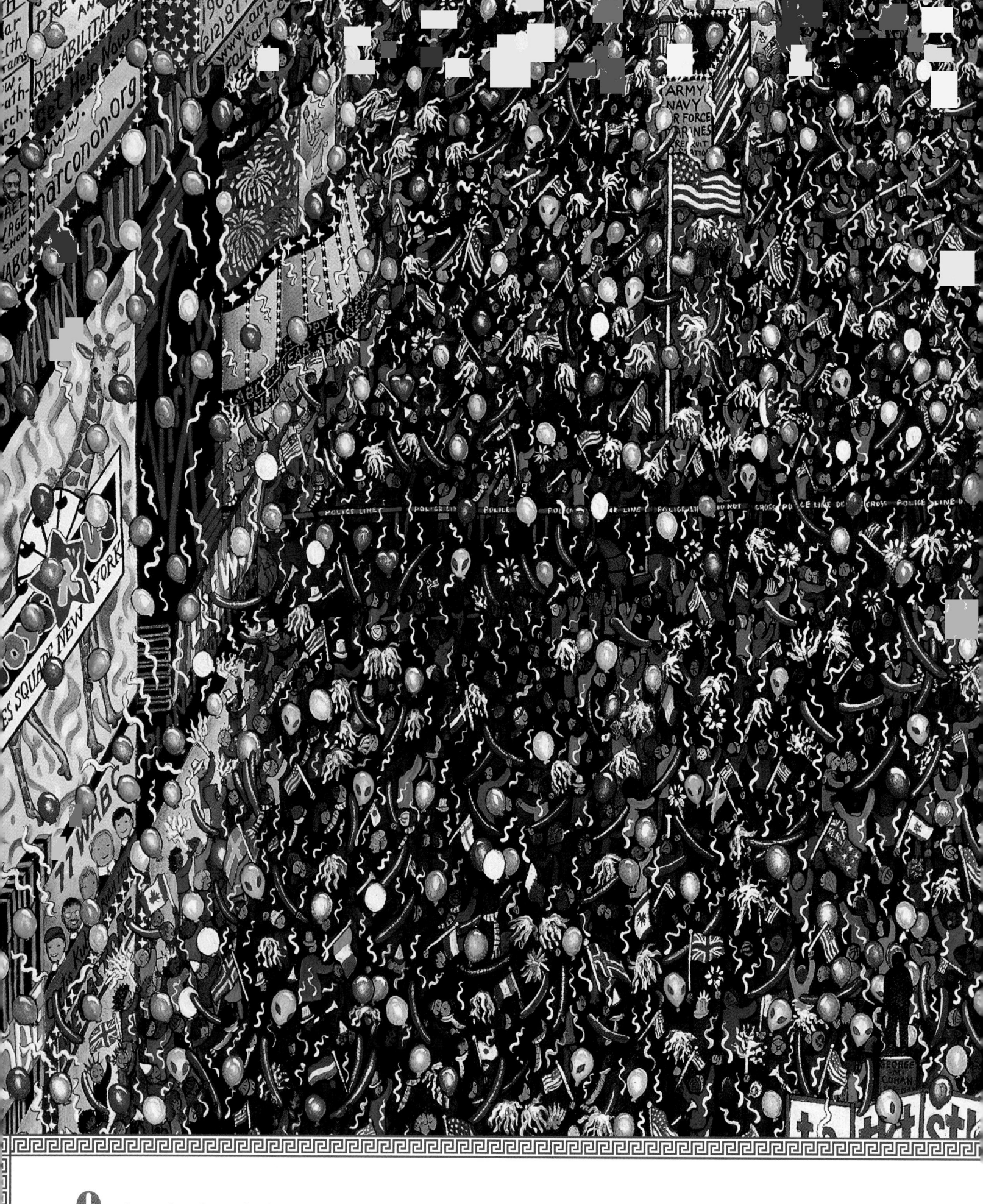

On the ticket I made for Martin, I drew people skating and the Prometheus statue and wrote:
ADMIT ONE STUDENT TO SKATING IN ROCKEFELLER CENTER. MERRY CHRISTMAS! HAPPY NEW YEAR!
We saw the New Year start together, on the roof deck of the Marriott Marquis Hotel in Times Square.
A minute before midnight, the countdown started. People shouted out the seconds, music played,
and confetti and balloons and fireworks filled the air. Martin and I shouted as loudly as we could,

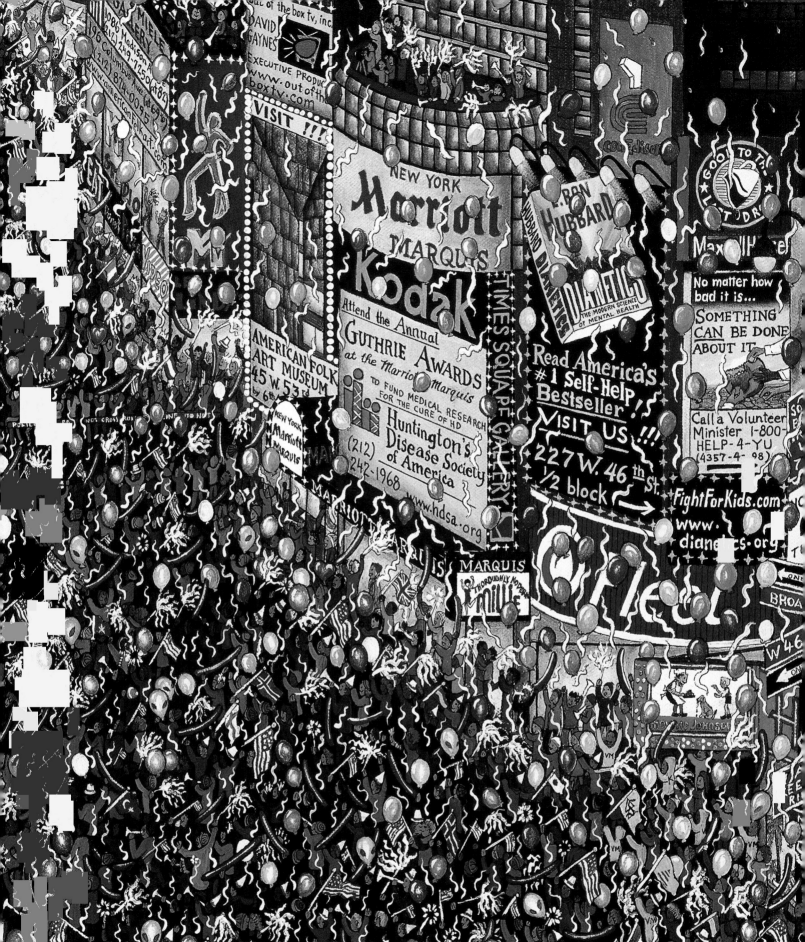

and then, as the ball dropped, everyone sang "Auld Lang Syne," and we did, too. Giant TV screens showed how people all over America and the world were watching Times Square at midnight in New York. I felt excited and proud to be right in the middle of it all—and to be a New Yorker.

So now you've seen *my* New York. Use the map and have fun exploring *your* New York!

FUN FACTS ABOUT NEW YORK
Plus a Reader's Challenge

Here are some of my favorite New York details, with their addresses. I challenge you to find them in this book's paintings. And I'm sure you noticed Speedy in some paintings, but maybe you didn't know that he is somewhere in each one. Sometimes he's very hard to see, but he's there. See if you can spot him!

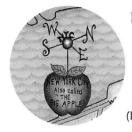

In New York, "downtown" means south and "uptown" means north. Fifth Avenue is the dividing line between the east and west sides of the city. Most numbered streets are one-way. In general, even-numbered streets go east and odd-numbered streets go west. (Remember: E for "east" and "even.")

FIFTH AVENUE AND 42ND STREET

The lions' original names were Lord Astor and Lady Lenox, after the founders of the library. In the 1930s, Mayor LaGuardia changed their names to Patience and Fortitude, because he said New Yorkers would need both to survive the Great Depression.

CENTRAL PARK, FIFTH AVENUE AND 64TH STREET

The seals in the zoo are fed fish twice a day during visiting hours. Call the zoo for times.

MIDDLE OF SOUTH CENTRAL PARK, NEAR 65TH STREET

The carousel has four horses per row. The largest are on the outside and they are three-quarters the size of a real horse.

EIGHTH AVENUE BETWEEN 30TH AND 31ST STREETS (OPPOSITE MADISON SQUARE GARDEN)

You can see more than 2,500 dogs at the Westminster Kennel Club Dog Show across the street from D'Aiuto's Bakery, New York New York Cheesecake. Show rings in Madison Square Garden are filled with dogs of all breeds for two days every February. Visit www.thepoop.com for the exact dates.

FULTON STREET

In England, some port cities had time balls that dropped exactly at noon, which nearby ships used to reset their clocks. Today in New York, we have two time balls. One drops at midnight in Times Square on New Year's Eve; another drops every day at noon in South Street Seaport.

WALL STREET

Wall Street is named for the wall the Dutch built in the 1600s to keep enemies out of the city.

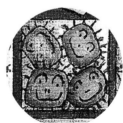

FIFTH AVENUE AND EAST 58TH STREET

The toys Becky drew are called Ducky Designs because her parents used to call her Ducky.

NEW YORK HARBOR

Fifteen-year-old Annie Moore from Ireland was the first immigrant admitted to the United States through Ellis Island in 1892.

42ND STREET AT LEXINGTON

Chrysler is a car company, and the building's spire was designed to look like the radiator grills on the old cars. There are real hubcaps on the sides of the building.

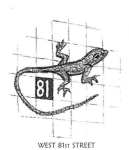

WEST 81ST STREET

Some of the subway animals are marked with a red-tiled question mark. This means that their species is endangered.

GREENWICH VILLAGE

There are two Halloween parades in Greenwich Village—one in the afternoon in Washinton Square for children and one at dusk on 6TH Avenue for adults.

125TH STREET BETWEEN SEVENTH AND EIGHTH AVENUES

Singers, dancers, musicians, comedians, and more perform at the Apollo Theater. Performers of any age can audition—each week, a few are picked to line up and take their turns in front of the audience on Amateur Night. Stevie Wonder, Ella Fitzgerald, and Louis Armstrong were all discovered there—you never know who might be next!

WEST 49TH STREET BETWEEN FIFTH AND SIXTH AVENUES

The gold statue is the Greek god Prometheus, who gave fire to man.

50TH STREET AND SIXTH AVENUE

Very early in the morning, the animals in the Living Nativity go outside for a walk with their trainer. Usually, she takes them around the Christmas tree; if you see them, you can feed them.

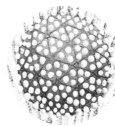

FIFTH AVENUE AT WEST 59TH STREET

A farm in Middleton, New York, gives old carriage horses a home. Their former drivers—and other people, too—can visit them, although no one can ride them. You can see photographs of the farm and the horses that live there on www.petsalive.com.

77TH STREET TO 34TH STREET

Macy's has been in Herald Square for more than 100 years. Its parade was the first big public celebration in New York designed for children.

42ND STREET AND BROADWAY

The sparkling ball that drops every New Year's Eve is made of 504 crystal triangles. Some are engraved with a new design each year, such as a star with seven points for the seven continents. People and animals from all seven, even Antarctica (remember the penguins!), live in New York City.

Extra Challenge: Try to find these items in this book!
Warning: these are really hard to find, so here's a hint: there's one object from every painting, starting with the New York Public Library page. Beware—these are not in order!

1
2
3
4
5
6
7
8
9
10
11
12
13
14
15
16
17
18
19
20
21
22
23
24
25
26
27
28

Stumped? See next page for answers.

There are some notable New Yorkers and other famous people in this book, too. See if you can recognize them!

Woody Allen
Brooke Astor
Art Bell
Michael Bloomberg
Liz Callaway
Bill, Hillary, and Chelsea Clinton
Judy Collins
Bob Dylan
Rudy Giuliani
Woody Guthrie
Rush Limbaugh
Demi Moore
Jerry Seinfeld
Curtis Sliwa
Liz Smith
John Travolta and Kelly Preston
Bruce Willis

Also illustrated by Kathy Jakobsen:

THIS LAND IS YOUR LAND

JOHNNY APPLESEED

Author's note:

I have taken some artistic license in this book, mostly in an effort to fit as much of New York City as I could into each page. Also, this city is always changing, but I tried to be as accurate as I possibly could. In some paintings you may notice little people with their names on balloons. These are friends and family and their pets. If any of my little painted people resemble you, you may claim them and be in the book, too! I hope you enjoy exploring New York City with Becky, Martin, and Speedy!

First Revised Edition

Library of Congress Cataloging-in-Publication Data

Jakobsen, Kathy.
    My New York / Kathy Jakobsen. — 1st rev. ed., New anniversary ed.
        p.   cm.
    Summary: Becky, a young New Yorker, takes the reader and a friend on a tour of her favorite places in the city.
    "Megan Tingley Books."
    ISBN 0-316-92711-2 / ISBN 0-316-71350-3 (holiday edition)
    1. New York (N.Y.) — Pictorial works — Juvenile literature.
2. New York (N.Y.) in art — Juvenile literature.   [1. New York (N.Y.) 2. Letters.]   I. Title.
[1. New York (N.Y.)]   I. Title
F128.37.J34   2003
974.7'1'00222 — dc21   2003040271

10 9 8 7 6 5 4 3 2 1

TWP

Printed in Singapore

The illustrations for this book were done in oil on canvas.
The text was set in Maiandra, and the display type is Binner Poster.

Answers to Extra Challenge:

1. MACY'S THANKSGIVING DAY PARADE: on front of Santa's sleigh   2. PLAZA HOTEL: in fountain   3. FRIEDSAM MEMORIAL CAROUSEL: to right of black horse, above balloons   4. THE RADIO CITY CHRISTMAS SPECTACULAR: left side, center   5. 81ST STREET SUBWAY: lower left corner   6. NEW YORK PUBLIC LIBRARY: lower right corner, on mailbox   7. RADIO CITY MUSIC HALL: center, on poster   8. CENTRAL PARK ZOO: in the penguin habitat   9. EMPIRE STATE BUILDING: lower right corner   10. CHINATOWN: upper right, dragon's tongue   11. GRAND CENTRAL TERMINAL/CHRYSLER BUILDING: bottom, right center, on bridge   12. D'AIUTO'S BAKERY: between Dobermans and shopkeepers   13. NEW YORK HARBOR ON THE FOURTH OF JULY: right side, under bridge   14. ANNEX ANTIQUES FAIR: lower right corner   15. FAO SCHWARZ: center, on clock tower   16. INTREPID: lower right corner   17. METROPOLITAN MUSEUM OF ART: on right side of steps, to left of balloons   18. STATUE OF LIBERTY: right side, center   19. THE NEW YORK CITY MARATHON: center, held by runner   20. THE VIEW FROM THE 86TH FLOOR OBSERVATORY: left corner of viewing platform   21. ROCKEFELLER CENTER: bottom center, near red bus   22. BAROSAURUS, AMERICAN MUSEUM OF NATURAL HISTORY: in glass case, left side, center   23. WALL STREET: window on Trinity Church   24. APOLLO THEATER: in upper right window   25. ROSE CENTER: to left of big sphere, below Jupiter   26. SOUTH STREET SEAPORT: upper left corner, under bridge   27. NEW YEAR'S EVE, TIMES SQUARE: center of yellow fireworks   28. WASHINGTON SQUARE PARK: lower left, fireman's hat

Answers to famous people:

title page: Giuliani, Bloomberg   NEW YORK PUBLIC LIBRARY, left to right: Seinfeld, Astor, Preston, Travolta, Callaway, Dylan, Guthrie, Collins, Allen, Willis, Moore.   D'AIUTO'S: Smith   FAO SCHWARZ: Limbaugh   ROSE CENTER: Bell   81ST STREET SUBWAY: Sliwa   APOLLO THEATER: Clintons